THE CHILDREN'S ILLUSTRATED TREASURY OF TRADITIONAL FIVE-MINUTE TALES

hinkler

THE CHILDREN'S ILLUSTRATED TREASURY

OF

TRADITIONAL FIVE-MINUTE TALES

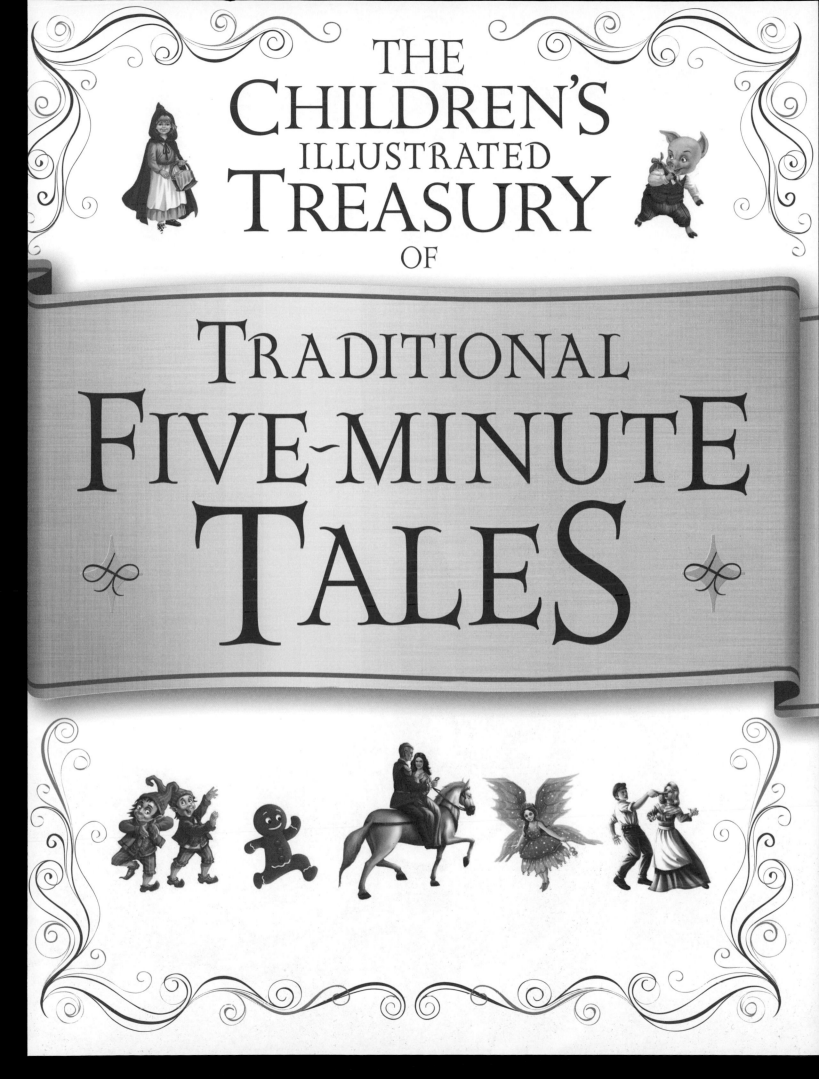

Published by Hinkler Books Pty Ltd
45–55 Fairchild Street
Heatherton Victoria 3202 Australia
www.hinkler.com.au

hinkler

© Hinkler Books Pty Ltd 2010, 2015

Editor: Suzannah Pearce
Cover design: Sam Grimmer
Internal design: Trudi Webb
Illustrators: Brijbasi Art Press Ltd
Designers: Diana Vlad, Susanna Murray and Paul Scott
Prepress: Graphic Print Group

ISBN 978 1 7428 1972 3

Printed and bound in China

CONTENTS

INTRODUCTION

For centuries, fairytales have given children their first taste of the world of books and literature. Not only are folk and fairytales rollicking good fun, whisking children away to worlds of magic and imagination, they also teach valuable lessons about how to make your way in a world that can be dark and challenging.

Our favourite fairytale characters don't always have an easy time. They meet and overcome obstacles at every turn, just as our children will – though, hopefully, not in the form of wicked witches or mischievous goblins.

Among the best-known collectors of European folklore and mythology were Jacob and Wilhelm Grimm, from Germany, and Hans Christian Andersen, from Denmark. Not only did they collect and publish fairytales that had been passed on through oral tradition for centuries, but Andersen, in particular, created original tales of his own. Several of these works are featured in this book.

A key feature of many fairytales is brevity, their authors aiming to encapsulate timeless lessons on life in short, sharp, memorable style. As the title suggests, the tales in *The Children's Illustrated Treasury of Five-Minute Tales* are intended to be read in around five minutes, and are great for the short attention spans of young children or busy parents. The fairytales can be enjoyed at bedtime, playtime, or whenever your family has five minutes to spare.

A love of reading and an appreciation of literature is one of the greatest gifts an adult can pass on to a child. Sharing fairytales with even the youngest children brings joy and delight and helps build and strengthen bonds of love, respect and understanding that can last a lifetime.

THE THREE LITTLE PIGS

Once upon a time there lived a mother sow with her
Three Little Pigs. As she did not have enough money to look
after them she sent them out into the world to seek their fortunes.

As he was walking down the road, the First Little Pig met a man
carrying a bundle of straw. 'Please, sir, give me that straw
so I can build a house with it.'

The man gave the straw to the First Little Pig, who went and
built a house with it.

As he was walking down the road, the Second Little Pig met a man carrying a bundle of sticks. 'Please, sir, give me those sticks so I can build a house with them.'

The man gave the sticks to the Second Little Pig, who went and built a house with them.

As he was walking down the road, the Third Little Pig met a man carrying a pile of bricks. 'Please, sir, give me those bricks so I can build a house with them.'

The man gave the bricks to the Third Little Pig, who went and built a house with them.

The Three Little Pigs lived happily until one day when a big bad Wolf came to the house of straw. The Wolf knocked at the door of the house made of straw and said, 'Little Pig, Little Pig, let me come in!'

The First Little Pig replied, 'No, not by the hair of my chinny chin chin!'

'Then I'll huff and I'll puff and I'll blow your house in!' cried the Wolf.

So the big bad Wolf huffed and he puffed and he blew down the house of straw. The First Little Pig ran as fast as he could to his brother's house of sticks.

Presently the big bad Wolf came to the house of sticks. The Wolf knocked at the door of the house made of sticks and said, 'Little Pig, Little Pig, let me come in!'

The First Little Pig and the Second Little Pig replied, 'No, not by the hair of my chinny chin chin!'

'Then I'll huff and I'll puff and I'll blow your house in!' cried the Wolf.

So the big bad Wolf huffed and he puffed and he huffed and he puffed and he blew down the house of sticks. The First Little Pig and the Second Little Pig ran as fast as they could to their brother's house of bricks.

Presently the big bad Wolf came to the house of bricks. The Wolf knocked at the door of the house made of bricks and said, 'Little Pig, Little Pig, let me come in!'

The First Little Pig and the Second Little Pig and the Third Little Pig replied, 'No, not by the hair of my chinny chin chin!'

'Then I'll huff and I'll puff and I'll blow your house in!' cried the Wolf.

So the big bad Wolf huffed and he puffed and he huffed and he puffed and he huffed and he puffed but he could not blow down the house of bricks.

When the Wolf realised that he could not blow down the house of bricks with his huffing and puffing, he said, 'Little Pig, I know where there is a nice field of juicy, tasty turnips.'

'Where?' asked the Third Little Pig.

'In Farmer Brown's field,' replied the Wolf. 'I will call for you at six o'clock tomorrow morning and we will go together to get some for our dinner.'

The next morning the clever Third Little Pig got up at five o'clock and went by himself to get the turnips. 'Are you ready to get some turnips?' asked the Wolf when he arrived at the Pig's house at six o'clock.

'Ready? I have already been and come back with a nice potful for my dinner!' replied the Third Little Pig.

The Wolf was very angry. He said, 'Little Pig, I know where there is a nice apple tree.'

'Where?' asked the Third Little Pig.

'In Farmer Smith's orchard,' replied the Wolf. 'I will call for you at five o'clock tomorrow morning, and we will go together to get some juicy, tasty apples.'

However, the clever Third Little Pig got up at four o'clock and went to the apple tree. As he had further to go he was still up the tree picking apples when he saw the angry Wolf coming.

'Little Pig come down and tell me if they are nice apples,' called the Wolf.

'They're very nice,' replied the Third Little Pig. 'Here, let me throw you one.' And he threw an apple so far that the Wolf had to go a long way to pick it up and the Little Pig was able to jump down and run home.

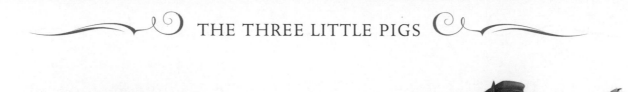

The next day the Wolf came and said to the Third Little Pig, 'Little Pig, there is a fair in town. Will you go with me at three o'clock this afternoon?'

'Very well,' said the Third Little Pig.

The Third Little Pig went off earlier to the fair and had a lovely time. He bought a butter churn and was heading home when he saw the Wolf coming. In a panic, he crawled inside the butter churn to hide and it fell over. Down the hill it rolled. When he saw the churn rolling towards him, the Wolf ran away in fright.

The Wolf went to the Third Little Pig's house and told him how he'd been frightened by a great round thing rolling down the hill towards him.

'Dear me, I hid inside the butter churn when I saw you coming and it rolled down the hill. I'm sorry I frightened you,' said the Third Little Pig.

The Wolf grew angry and swore that he would come down the chimney and eat up the First Little Pig and the Second Little Pig and the Third Little Pig. But while he was climbing on to the roof, the Third Little Pig made a blazing fire and put a big pot of water on to boil. As the Wolf was climbing down the chimney the Third Little Pig took off the lid and – splash! – the Wolf fell into the scalding water.

The Wolf howled and leapt so high that he jumped right out of the chimney. He ran off down the road as fast as he could. The Three Little Pigs lived happily ever after in the house of bricks and never saw the big bad Wolf again.

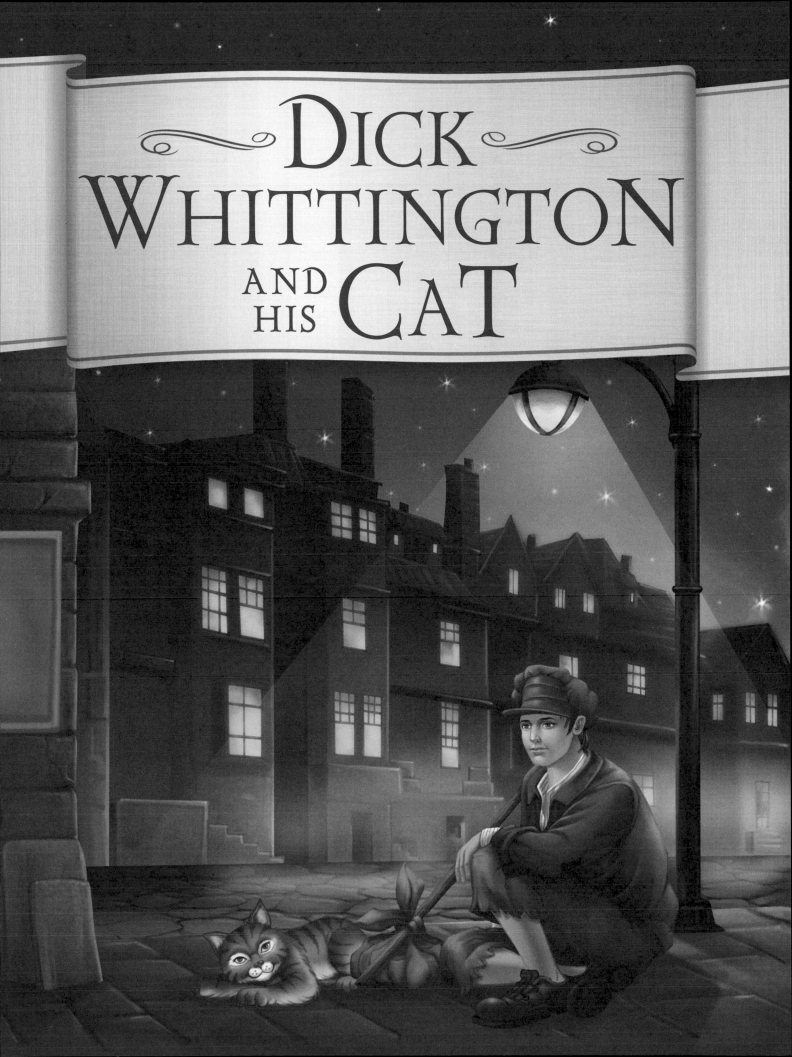

DICK WHITTINGTON
AND HIS CAT

Many years ago, there lived a boy named Dick Whittington. His parents died when he was very young, so he was very badly off. In those days country folk thought that the people of London were fine ladies and gentlemen who were so rich that the streets were paved with gold. Dick sat and listened to all these strange tales and longed to go to London and have fine clothes and lots to eat.

One day, a wagon with eight horses stopped in the village. Dick begged the driver to take him to London. The man felt sorry for Dick when he saw how ragged and poor he was. He agreed to take Dick, and they set off immediately.

Soon Dick found himself in the wonderful city he had heard so much about. But how disappointed he was! How dirty it seemed! He wandered up and down the streets, but not one was paved with gold. Instead, there was dirt everywhere.

Dick walked until it was dark. He sat down in a corner and fell asleep. When morning came, he was very cold and hungry, and although he asked everyone he met for help, only one or two gave him a halfpenny to buy some bread. For days, he lived on the streets, trying to find some work.

One day, he lay down in the doorway of a rich merchant named Fitzwarren. He was spotted by the cook, who was an unkind, bad-tempered woman. She cried out, 'Be off, lazy rogue, or I'll throw boiling hot, dirty dishwater over you!'

At that moment, Mr Fitzwarren came home for dinner. When he saw what was happening, he asked Dick why he had been lying there. 'You're old enough to work, my boy,' he said. 'I'm afraid you're just lazy.'

'But sir, that is not so,' Dick said. He told Mr Fitzwarren about his attempts to find work and described how hungry he was. Poor Dick was so weak that when he tried to stand, he fell down again. When the kind merchant saw this, he ordered that Dick be taken inside and given a good dinner. He said that Dick could stay and work in the kitchen, helping the cook.

Dick would have been happy if it weren't for the bad-tempered cook. She did her best to make life hard for Dick. She scolded him. Nothing he did was good enough. She even beat him with the broomstick or the ladle, or whatever else she had handy.

At last Miss Alice, Mr Fitzwarren's daughter, heard how badly the cook was treating Dick. She told the cook that she would lose her job if she didn't treat him more kindly, for the family had become quite fond of Dick.

After that the cook treated Dick better, but he had another problem. He slept in an attic that was overrun with rats and mice every night. Sometimes he hardly slept a wink. Luckily, one day he earned a penny for cleaning a gentleman's shoes. He then met a girl holding a cat and bought it with the penny. Puss soon saw that he had no more trouble with rats and mice, and he slept soundly every night.

One day, Mr Fitzwarren had a ship ready to sail. It was his custom to give his servants a chance to make their fortune, so he asked them what they wanted to send out on the ship to sell. They all had something to send except Dick, who had nothing. Miss Alice said, 'I will provide something for him,' but her father told her that it must be something of his own.

'I have nothing but my cat, which I bought for a penny,' Dick said.

'Go and fetch your cat then,' said Mr Fitzwarren.

Dick fetched poor Puss. There were tears in his eyes when he gave her to the ship's captain. They laughed at his odd goods, but Miss Alice, who felt sorry for him, gave Dick some money to buy another cat.

Miss Alice's acts of kindness made the cook jealous and she treated Dick worse than ever. She made fun of him for sending his cat to sea. 'Maybe the cat will sell for enough money to buy a stick to beat you with!' she mocked.

At last Dick could bear it no longer and ran away. He walked for a while and then sat down to rest. While he was sitting, the bells of the Bow Church began to chime. As they rang, it seemed they were singing over and over:

'Turn again, Whittington, Lord Mayor of London.'

'Lord Mayor of London!' he thought. 'Why, I'd put up with almost anything for that. I'll go back and ignore the nasty old cook.'
And back he went.

Meanwhile, the ship travelled far away until it came to a foreign harbour where they had never seen a ship from England before. The King invited the captain to the palace for dinner, but no sooner were they seated than a horde of rats swarmed over the dishes and started devouring the food.

Thinking of the cat, the captain said he had a creature that would take care of the rats. The King was eager to see this wonderful animal. 'Bring it to me,' he said, 'for the vermin are unbearable. If it does what you say, I will load your ship with treasure.'

When the captain returned with Puss, the floor was still covered with rats. When she saw them, puss jumped down. In no time at all, most of the rats were dead and the rest ran off in fright. The King was delighted.

The King bought all the ship's cargo and gave the captain ten times as much for the cat as all the rest together.

Mr Fitzwarren was at his counting house when he heard a knock. It was the ship's captain with a chest of jewels. The captain told him about the cat and showed him the riches. Mr Fitzwarren told his servants to bring Dick but the servants hesitated, saying so great a treasure was too much for Dick. Good Mr Fitzwarren cried, 'Nonsense! The treasure belongs to him!'

He sent for Dick, who was black with dirt from scouring pots. At first, Dick thought they must be making fun of him. He begged them not to play tricks on a poor boy.

'We are not joking,' said the merchant. 'The captain has sold your cat and brings you more riches than I possess. Long may you enjoy them!'

Dick begged his master and Miss Alice to accept a share, but thcy refused. Dick was far too kind-hearted to keep it all to himself, so he gave some to the captain, the mate and the rest of Mr Fitzwarren's servants, and even to his old enemy, the cook.

Mr Fitzwarren advised him to send for some gentleman's clothes, and told him he was welcome to live in his house until he could find his own. When Dick's face was washed and he was dressed in a smart suit, he was as handsome and fine as any man who visited fair Alice Fitzwarren. She soon fell in love with him, and he with her.

A day for the wedding was arranged. They were married and afterwards treated everyone to a magnificent feast. History tells us that Mr Whittington and his lady lived in great splendour and were very happy. He became Sheriff, was made Lord Mayor of London four times, and received the honour of knighthood from the King.

GOLDILOCKS
AND THE
THREE BEARS

Once upon a time there were three bears who lived together in a house in the woods. One of them was a Father Bear, one was a Mother Bear and the other was a Baby Bear.

They each had a bowl for their porridge: a big bowl for Father Bear, a medium-sized bowl for Mother Bear and a little bowl for Baby Bear. They each had a chair to sit on: a big chair for Father Bear, a medium-sized chair for Mother Bear and a little chair for Baby Bear. And they each had a bed to sleep in: a big bed for Father Bear, a medium-sized bed for Mother Bear and a little bed for Baby Bear.

One day, they made their porridge for breakfast and poured it into the porridge bowls. They decided to go for a walk in the woods while their porridge was cooling so they wouldn't burn their mouths. After all, they were sensible, well-brought-up bears.

While the bears were out walking, a little girl called Goldilocks passed by. She lived on the other side of the woods and had been sent on an errand by her mother. She saw the house and looked in the window. Goldilocks knocked on the door and then bent down and peered in the keyhole. She could see that no one was at home, so she lifted the latch and walked in.

Goldilocks was very pleased when she saw the bowls of porridge sitting on the table. Of course, most people would wait for the bears to come home and hope to be invited to breakfast. However, Goldilocks was rather spoiled and badly brought up, so she set about helping herself.

First she tried Father Bear's porridge, but that was too hot. Next she tried Mother Bear's porridge, but that was too cold. Then she tried Baby Bear's porridge, and that was neither too hot nor too cold. It was just right. Goldilocks liked it so much that she ate it all up.

Then Goldilocks felt tired, so she was pleased when she saw the three chairs. First she tried Father Bear's chair, but that was too hard. Next she tried Mother Bear's chair, but that was too soft. Then she tried Baby Bear's chair, and that was neither too hard nor too soft. It was just right. Goldilocks liked it so much that she sat in it until the chair gave way and she crashed down to the ground. That made her very cross.

Goldilocks was still feeling very tired, so she went upstairs to the bedroom, where she found the three beds. First she tried Father Bear's bed, but that was too hard. Next she tried Mother Bear's bed, but that was too soft. Then she tried Baby Bear's bed, and that was neither too hard nor too soft. It was just right. Goldilocks liked it so much that she pulled the covers over herself and fell fast asleep.

By this time, the three bears thought their porridge would be cool enough and came home to breakfast. When they went to the table, they saw that someone had left the spoons sitting in the porridge.

'Someone has been eating my porridge!' shouted Father Bear.

'Someone has been eating my porridge!' exclaimed Mother Bear.

'Someone has been eating my porridge, and they've eaten it all up!' cried Baby Bear.

The bears realised that somebody had been in their house, so they looked around to see if anything else had been disturbed. When they looked at the chairs, they saw that someone had moved the cushions on the seats around.

'Someone has been sitting in my chair!' shouted Father Bear.

'Someone has been sitting in my chair!' exclaimed Mother Bear.

'Someone has been sitting in my chair, and it's all broken!' cried Baby Bear.

The bears searched further, in case it was a burglar who had been in their house. They went upstairs to their bedroom and saw that the bedclothes on the beds were in disarray.

'Someone has been sleeping in my bed!' shouted Father Bear.

'Someone has been sleeping in my bed!' exclaimed Mother Bear.

'Someone has been sleeping in my bed, and they're still there!' cried Baby Bear.

Goldilocks got a terrible fright when she woke up and saw the three bears standing by the bed, looking at her. She jumped out of the other side of the bed and ran to the open window. She jumped out of the window and landed on the soft, springy grass below. She ran home as fast as she could.

The three bears never saw Goldilocks again, but she learnt her lesson about respecting the belongings of others. And the bears cooked a fresh batch of porridge and had their tasty breakfast!

THE
STEADFAST
TIN SOLDIER

There were once twenty-five tin soldiers. They were brothers, for they had all been made out of the same piece of tin. They each stood tall and looked straight ahead and wore a splendid red and blue uniform.

The first thing in the world they ever heard were the words, 'Tin soldiers!'. The words were uttered by an excited little boy, who clapped his hands in delight when he opened the lid of the box in which the soldiers lay. They were a birthday present.

The little boy set them up on the table. They were exactly alike, apart from one who only had one leg. He had been made last and there was not quite enough melted tin to finish him, so they made him stand firmly on one leg, which made him quite remarkable.

The table on which the tin soldiers stood was covered with other playthings, but the most attractive was a pretty paper castle. Through the small windows the rooms could be seen. A number of trees stood in front of the castle, around a small mirror, which was intended to represent a lake.

This was very pretty, but the prettiest of all was a tiny little lady standing near the open door of the castle. She was also made of paper and she wore a dress of sheer gauze with a narrow blue ribbon over her shoulders like a scarf. On her dress was fastened a glittering tinsel rose, as large as her face. The little lady was a dancer. She stretched out both her arms and raised one of her legs so high that the little Tin Soldier could not see it at all, and so he thought that she, like himself, only had one leg.

'This is the wife for me,' the Tin Soldier thought, 'but she is too grand and lives in a castle. I only have a box to live in with five and twenty of us together. That is no place for her. But still, I must try and make her acquaintance.' The Tin Soldier laid himself out at full length on the table behind a snuff box so that he could peep at the delicate paper lady, who continued to stand on one leg without losing her balance.

When the evening came, the other tin soldiers were all placed in their box and the people of the house went to bed. Then the playthings began to have their own games together. They paid visits, wrestled and went to balls. The Tin Soldiers rattled in their box; they wanted to get out and join the fun but they could not open the lid. The nutcrackers played leapfrog and the pencils jumped around the table. There was so much noise that the canary woke up and began to quote poetry.

With all this activity, only the Tin Soldier and the Dancer remained in their places. She stood on tiptoe, her legs stretched out, as firmly as the soldier stood on his one leg. He never took his eyes off her, even for a moment. Then the clock struck twelve and, with a bounce, up sprung the lid of the snuff box. Instead of snuff, a little goblin jumped up, for the snuff box was a prank: it was really a jack-in-the-box.

'Tin Soldier,' said the goblin. 'Don't wish for the impossible.'

But the Tin Soldier pretended not to hear.

'Very well, wait until tomorrow then,' said the goblin.

The next morning, the children placed the Tin Soldier in the window. Now, whether it was the goblin's magic or the wind, it is not known, but the window flew open and out fell the little soldier, head over heels, from the third storey into the street. It was a terrible fall, for he came down headfirst, and his helmet and bayonet were stuck between the stones with his leg in the air.

The maid and the little boy went down to try and find him but he was nowhere to be seen.

Soon it began to rain. The drops fell faster and faster, until it was a heavy shower. When it was over, two boys came along and one of them said, 'Look, there is a tin soldier. He should have a boat to sail in.'

They made a boat out of newspaper and put the soldier in it.

The boys sent the boat down the stream of rainwater in the gutter, while they ran alongside clapping. The waves in the gutter were very high and the stream rolled along quickly. The boat rocked up and down and spun around so quickly that the soldier trembled, but his expression did not change. Suddenly the boat shot into a tunnel, and it was as dark as the Tin Soldier's box.

'Where am I going now?' thought the soldier. 'I am sure this is the goblin's fault. If only the little lady were here with me, I should not mind the darkness.'

Suddenly a water rat who lived in the drain appeared before him. 'Where is your passport?' asked the water rat. 'Show it to me at once.'

But the Tin Soldier stayed stiff and silent. The boat sailed on and the rat followed, crying out, 'Stop him!'

The stream rushed on stronger and stronger. Now the Tin Soldier could see daylight ahead and he heard a roaring sound loud enough to frighten the strongest man.

At the end of the tunnel, the drain emptied into a canal down a steep gutter, which was as dangerous for him as a waterfall was for a person. The boat rushed on and the poor Tin Soldier could only hold himself as stiffly as possible, without moving an eyelid, to show he wasn't afraid.

The boat was swept over. It whirled around three or four times, and then filled with water. Nothing could stop it from sinking. The Tin Soldier was up to his neck in water as the newspaper became soft and loose, until at last the water closed over his head. As he sank, he thought of the elegant little Dancer who he would never see again.

The boat fell apart and the soldier plunged down into the water, but immediately afterwards he was swallowed up by a large fish. Oh, how dark it was inside the fish's belly! It was darker and narrower than the tunnel, but still the Tin Soldier stood firm.

The fish swam to and fro, but eventually it became quite still. After a while, a flash of light seemed to pass through it and then daylight appeared. A voice cried out, 'Oh, I do declare! Here is the Tin Soldier!'

The fish had been caught, taken to market and sold to the cook. They placed him on a table. How strange it was to be in the same room with the same children, the same playthings, the same table and the pretty castle with the pretty Dancer at the door! She was still balancing on one leg, as unrelenting as himself.

It moved the Tin Soldier so much to see her that he almost wept, but he held back. He looked at her and they both remained silent.

Suddenly one of the boys picked up the Tin Soldier and threw him into the stove for no reason. The flames lit up the little Tin Soldier and the heat was terrible, but whether it was from the fire or from love, he could not say. He looked at the little lady and she looked at him. He started to melt away, but he remained steadfast, with his arms at his side.

Suddenly a draught of air picked up the little Dancer. She fluttered like a fairy right into the stove by the Tin Soldier's side. She instantly burst into flames and was gone. The Tin Soldier melted down into a lump and the next morning, as the maid was cleaning out the stove, she found him melted into the shape of a little tin heart. Nothing remained of the little Dancer but the tinsel rose, which was burnt as black as a cinder.

Rumpelstiltskin

Once upon a time there lived a poor miller who had a beautiful daughter. Now, it happened that the King often hunted in the woods near the miller's village. The foolish miller, trying to make himself appear more important, told the King that his daughter could spin straw into gold.

'Now, that's a talent worth having,' said the King, who was very fond of money. 'Bring her to my palace tomorrow and I'll put her to the test.'

The next day, the miller's daughter was brought before the King. He led her to a room that was full of straw, gave her a spinning wheel and said, 'Now, set to work and spin all night. If you haven't spun this straw into gold by dawn, you shall die.'

The poor girl protested in vain. The door was locked and she was left alone. She sat down and began to cry, as she had no way of turning the straw into gold. Suddenly the door opened and a strange little man stepped into the room.

'Good day to you, young lass,' the man said. 'What are you weeping for?'

'Alas!' the miller's daughter replied, 'I must spin this straw into gold and I do not know how.'

'What would you give me to do it for you?' asked the strange little man.

'My necklace,' replied the girl.

The little man took the necklace and sat down at the spinning wheel. 'Whir, whir,' went the wheel as the little man sat and spun. He whistled and sang as he worked:

'Round about, round about. Lo and behold!

Reel away, reel away, straw into gold!'

Soon the work was done and all the straw was spun into gold.

When the King came in the next morning and saw the pile of gold, he was astonished and pleased. However, his greed for gold grew stronger. He put the miller's daughter in a room with a larger pile of straw and told her that if she valued her life, she must spin it all into gold by the next morning.

Once again, the miller's daughter sat down and burst into tears.

But then, as before, the door opened and in walked the strange little man.

'What will you give me if I complete your task?' he asked the miller's daughter.

'The ring on my finger,' answered the girl.

The little man took the ring and sat down at the spinning wheel. 'Whir, whir,' went the wheel again. The little man sat and spun, whistling and singing as he worked:

'Round about, round about. Lo and behold!

Reel away, reel away, straw into gold!'

Before morning, the little man had finished and all the straw was spun into gold.

The King came in the next morning and was even more pleased with the pile of gold. However, his greed was not satisfied. He took the miller's daughter into a room with an even larger pile of straw and said, 'All this must be spun tonight. If it is, you shall become my Queen.'

As soon as the girl was alone, the little man came in and asked, 'What will you give me if I spin for you a third time?'

'I have nothing left to give,' she replied.

'Then promise you'll give me your first child when you are Queen,' said the strange little man.

'That may never come to pass,' thought the girl, 'but if I do not promise, I have no way of finishing this task.'

So she promised the little man her first-born child and he set about spinning the straw into gold. He spun away and sang:

'Round about, round about. Lo and behold!

Reel away, reel away, straw into gold!'

When the King came in the next morning, he was delighted with the pile of gold. Straight away he married the miller's daughter and she became Queen.

When her first child was born, the Queen was very happy. She had forgotten the little man and her promise.

Then one day, while she was sitting playing with the baby, the little man walked into the room and reminded her of her promise.

She sobbed and cried, begging him to free her from the promise. She offered him all the treasures in the kingdom, but the little man refused. Finally, her tears softened his heart and he said, 'I will give you three days. If you can guess my name during that time, you can keep the child.'

The Queen lay awake all night, trying to think what his name could be. She sent out messengers all over the land to find any names they could.

The next day, the little man returned and she began with all the names she could think of: Timothy, Melchior, Balthazar, Benjamin, Jeremiah and more. To all of them, he replied, 'That is not my name.'

On the second day, she sent servants out to gather all the names in the neighbourhood and had a long list of unusual and comic names: Bandylegs, Crookshanks, Hunchback and more. Still he replied, 'That is not my name.'

On the third day, as the Queen was starting to despair, one of the messengers came back. He told the Queen, 'I travelled for two days without hearing any new names, but yesterday, as I was climbing a high hill in the forest, I saw a little hut. Before the hut was a fire and around the fire a strange little man was dancing and singing:

'Today I brew, tomorrow I bake,

And the royal child I'll take.

Little does my lady dream

That Rumpelstiltskin is my name!'

The Queen jumped for joy when she heard this. When the little man came in, she asked him, 'Is your name Conrad?'

'That is not my name.'

'Is your name Lincoln?'

'That is not my name.'

'Is your name Rumpelstiltskin?'

'Some witch or devil has told you that!' the little man screamed angrily. He stamped his foot so hard that he fell through the floor up to his waist, and was forced to use both hands to pull himself out. Then the strange little man ran out of the room, leaving the child with the Queen, and was never seen or heard of again.

THE
WOLF AND THE
SEVEN LITTLE KIDS

There was once a goat who had Seven Little Kids. She loved them all, just as much as any mother loves her children. One day, she had to go into the woods to get some food for them all.

The Mother goat called all her children to her and told them, 'Dear children, I have to go into the woods. Now, do not open the door while I am away. You must be on guard for the Wolf. If he gets in, he will eat all of you up, and not even a hair would be left. The Wolf often tries to disguise himself, but you will recognise him at once by his rough voice and his black feet.'

'Mother dear, we will be very careful not to let the old Wolf in!' the Seven Little Kids cried. 'There is no need to worry about us.' So the Mother goat bleated and went on her way with her mind at ease.

It was not long before there was a loud knock at the door and a voice cried out, 'Open the door, my dear children! It is your Mother and I have brought something back for each of you.'

But the Little Kids knew from the rough voice that it was the Wolf at the door.

'We will not open the door!' they called out. 'You are not our Mother! Our Mother's voice is soft and gentle. Your voice is rough and hard. You are a Wolf!'

The old Wolf ran to a shop and bought himself a large piece of chalk, which he ate to make his voice soft, twisting his face up at the nasty taste. Then he went back and knocked at the door, calling out in his soft voice, 'Open the door, dear children! It is your Mother and I have brought something back for each of you.'

But the Wolf had laid one of his black paws on the window sill. The Seven Little Kids saw it and cried out, 'We will not open the door! You are not our Mother! Our Mother's feet are white. Yours are black. You are a Wolf!'

The old Wolf ran to the baker and said to him, 'Mr Baker, put some dough on my foot, for I have sprained it.'

After the baker had rubbed dough on his foot, the Wolf went to the miller and said, 'Sprinkle some white flour on my foot.'

The miller thought to himself, 'The Wolf wants to trick someone,' and refused to do it. But the Wolf said, 'If you will not do it, I will eat you up.' That frightened the miller, so he did as the Wolf asked and sprinkled white flour on his paw.

Then the Wolf went back to the goat's house and knocked on the door. He called out in his soft voice, 'Open the door, dear children! It is your Mother.'

The Seven Little Kids cried out, 'First, show us your foot!' So the Wolf put his one white foot on the window sill. When the Seven Little Kids saw that the foot was white, they thought it must be their Mother and opened the door. But no! It was the Wolf!

All the Little Kids ran to hide themselves. The first hid under the table, the second in the bed, the third in the oven, the fourth in the kitchen, the fifth in the cupboard, the sixth under the washbasin and the seventh, who was the smallest of all, in the grandfather clock. The Wolf quickly found them and gobbled them up. However, he did not find the youngest kid, who was in the clock.

After he had satisfied his appetite, the Wolf felt very sleepy. He went outside and found some green grass under a tree in the meadow. He lay down and went to sleep.

A little later, the Mother goat came back from the woods. The door was wide open, the tables and chairs were turned over, the washing bowl lay broken in pieces and the bedding had been torn off the bed. She looked for her children but none were to be seen. She called them by name, one after the other, but there was no answer until she came to the youngest. Then a soft voice cried out, 'Mother dear, I am hiding in the clock!'

The Mother goat rescued the youngest kid from the clock and learned how the Wolf had eaten her dear children. She went outside and saw the Wolf in the meadow, fast asleep on the grass. As the goat looked at the Wolf, she saw that his belly was jumping and jiggling.

'Goodness!' she thought. 'Is it possible that my poor children are still alive?'

The Mother goat sent the youngest kid inside to get a pair of scissors and a needle and thread. She quickly cut a hole in the Wolf's belly. At the first snip of the scissors, one of the kids stuck its head out of the hole. She cut a little more and one after the other, all six jumped out. They had suffered no injury whatsoever! They hugged their Mother and jumped about on the grass.

The Mother goat said, 'Quick, go and look for some big stones from the stream!'

The Seven Little Kids ran off to the stream and soon came back with seven large stones. They put the stones in the Wolf's belly and the Mother goat sewed the Wolf up so gently and quietly that he did not wake up or move.

At last the Wolf woke, feeling very thirsty. He stood up and the stones in his belly began to rattle and bump against each other. He walked slowly to the stream to drink, but when he bent over, the stones were so heavy that they tipped him over into the deep water. He sank without a trace and the Seven Little Kids danced for joy, singing, 'The Wolf is gone! The Wolf is gone!'. The Mother goat hugged her Seven Little Kids and they all lived happily, and safely, ever after.

THE LITTLE RED HEN

The Little Red Hen lived in the barnyard with her chicks. She spent her time walking about in her picketty-pecketty way, scratching the ground and looking for worms to feed her family. She loved juicy, fat worms and whenever she found one, she would call out 'Chuck-chuck-chuck!' to her chicks, who would come running. She would share out her find and then it was back to her picketty-pecketty scratching, looking for more.

A Cat usually napped lazily away next to the barn door in the sun, not even bothering to chase the Rat, who ran here and there as he pleased. As for the Pig who lived in the sty, he did not care about anything, as long as he could eat and get fat.

One summer day as she was scratching away, the Little Red Hen found a seed sitting in the dust. She discovered it was a wheat seed. If it was planted, it would grow seeds that could be made into flour and turned into bread.

The Little Red Hen thought of the Cat, who slept all day, and the Rat, who did as he pleased, and the Pig, whose only concern was his food. She called out loudly to them, 'Who will plant this seed?'

But the Cat meowed, 'Not I,' and the Rat squeaked, 'Not I,' and the Pig grunted, 'Not I.'

'Well then,' said the Little Red Hen, 'I will.'

And she did.

Then she went about her duties, scratching for worms in her picketty-pecketty way and feeding her chicks, while the Cat grew fat, and the Rat grew fat, and the Pig grew fat. Meanwhile, the wheat grew tall.

One day, the Little Red Hen decided that the wheat was grown and ripe, ready for harvest. She called out loudly, 'Who will harvest the wheat?'

But the Cat meowed, 'Not I,' and the Rat squeaked, 'Not I,' and the Pig grunted, 'Not I.'

'Well then,' said the Little Red Hen, 'I will.'

And she did.

She went and got the farmer's sickle from his tools in the barn and harvested the wheat in her picketty-pecketty way. The nicely cut wheat lay on the ground, but her little yellow chicks crowded around her, 'peep-peep-peeping' for attention, crying that their mother was neglecting them.

Poor Little Red Hen! She didn't know what to do. She was divided between her duty to her chicks and her duty to the wheat. So, hoping for some help, she called out, 'Who will thresh the wheat?'

But the Cat meowed, 'Not I,' and the Rat squeaked, 'Not I,' and the Pig grunted, 'Not I.'

'Well then,' said the Little Red Hen, 'I will.'

And she did.

Of course, she first went a-hunting worms for her children and made sure that they were all fed and happy. When they were all asleep for their afternoon nap, she went out and threshed the wheat.

Then she called out, 'Who will carry the wheat to the mill to be ground into flour?'

But the Cat meowed, 'Not I,' and the Rat squeaked, 'Not I,' and the Pig grunted, 'Not I.'

'Well then,' said the Little Red Hen, 'I will.'

And she did.

The Little Red Hen loaded up the wheat in a sack and headed off to the mill, far away. The miller ground her wheat into beautiful flour and she trudged back again in her picketty-pecketty way. She even managed, in spite of the load, to catch a juicy worm or two for her chicks. She was so tired when she returned that she went to sleep early.

The Little Red Hen would have loved to sleep late but her chicks woke her, 'peep-peep-peeping' for their breakfast. As she woke, she remembered that today was the day to make the flour into bread. After her children were fed, she went looking for the Cat, the Rat and the Pig. She called out, 'Who will make the bread?'

But the Cat meowed, 'Not I,' and the Rat squeaked, 'Not I,' and the Pig grunted, 'Not I.'

'Well then,' said the Little Red Hen, 'I will.'

And she did.

She put on a fresh apron and a white cook's hat and followed the recipe. She made the dough and kneaded it and shaped it into loaves and put them in the oven to bake.

At last, the bread was ready. A delicious smell wafted across the barnyard. The Cat, the Rat and the Pig all sniffed the air with delight. The Little Red Hen went over to the oven in her picketty-pecketty way. She was very excited about the wonderful bread, which is not surprising, for had she not done all the work?

The Little Red Hen opened the oven and found that the lovely brown loaves of bread were cooked to perfection. Then, out of habit, she called out, 'Who will eat the bread?'

And the Cat meowed, 'I will,' and the Rat squeaked, 'I will,' and the Pig grunted, 'I will.'

But the Little Red Hen said, 'No, you won't. I will.'

And she did!

THE
PRINCESS
AND THE PEA

There once lived a Prince who wished to marry a Princess. However, she had to be a real Princess.

The Prince travelled all over the world, searching for such a lady, but there was always something wrong. He found Princesses in abundance, but it seemed impossible for him to tell whether they were real Princesses. There always seemed to be something not quite right about the ladies. Finally, the Prince returned home alone to his palace, quite downcast, as he wished so much to have a real Princess for his wife.

One evening, there was a terrible storm. The rain poured down in torrents, lightning cracked across the sky and thunder crashed loudly. It was pitch dark and the wind howled. Suddenly, there was a great knocking at the palace door, and the King, the Prince's father, went to open it.

When he opened the door, the King saw a Princess standing there. The rain and the wind had left her in a sad condition. Her clothes were soaked through and clung to her, and the water trickled down her hair and face. The old King showed the Princess inside and she told him that she was a real Princess.

'Indeed! We'll soon see if that's true!' thought the Prince's mother, the Queen. However, she didn't say a word to anyone about what she was planning to do. She went to the bed in the guest bedroom and rolled the bedclothes and the mattress away. The Queen laid a little pea on the bed frame and replaced the mattress and the bedclothes.

Then the Queen ordered that twenty mattresses be laid one on top of the other over the pea. Next she ordered that twenty feather eiderdowns be laid over the twenty mattresses. This was the bed where the Princess was to sleep.

The next morning, the Queen asked the Princess how she had slept.

'Oh, very badly indeed!' exclaimed the Princess. 'I barely closed my eyes the whole night through. I do not know what was in my bed, but there was definitely something hard underneath me. I am all bruised black and blue. It has hurt me so much!'

Now the Queen knew that this Princess was, indeed, a real Princess because she had felt the pea through twenty mattresses and twenty feather eiderdowns. Only a real Princess could be so delicate and sensitive.

The Prince was overjoyed and married her, for he knew that his wife was a real Princess. As for the pea, it is said that it is kept in the castle in a cabinet of curiosities, where it can still be seen today.

The Royal Pea

THE GINGERBREAD MAN

There was once a little old man and a little old woman who lived in a little old house on the edge of a wood. They would have been a very happy little old couple but for one thing – they had no little child and they wished for one very much.

One day, the little old woman was baking gingerbread. She cut the dough in the shapes of little boys. They had currants for eyes and cherries for buttons. The little old woman put them into the oven.

After a little while, the little old woman went to the oven to see if they were baked. As soon as she opened the oven door, one little gingerbread man jumped out and began to run away as fast as he could!

The little old woman called out to her husband. They both ran after the little Gingerbread Man, but he was so fast that they could not catch him. As he ran, he sang out:

'Run, run as fast as you can!

You can't catch me,

I'm the Gingerbread Man!'

Soon the Gingerbread Man came to a barn full of workers who were threshing wheat. He called out to them as he ran past, saying:

'I've run away from a little old woman,

A little old man,

And I can run away from you, I can!

Run, run as fast as you can!

You can't catch me,

I'm the Gingerbread Man!'

The barn full of threshers all ran after the Gingerbread Man. Although they ran fast, they could not catch him.

The little Gingerbread Man ran on until he came to a field full of mowers. He called out to them:

'I've run away from a little old woman,

A little old man,

A barn full of threshers,

And I can run away from you, I can!

Run, run as fast as you can!

You can't catch me,

I'm the Gingerbread Man!'

The mowers all ran after the Gingerbread Man, but they couldn't catch him.

The little Gingerbread Man ran on until he came to a cow. He shouted out to her:

'I've run away from a little old woman,

A little old man,

A barn full of threshers,

A field full of mowers,

And I can run away from you, I can!

Run, run as fast as you can!

You can't catch me,

I'm the Gingerbread Man!'

The cow ran after the Gingerbread Man, but she couldn't catch him.

The little Gingerbread Man ran on until he came to a pig.
He cried out to the pig:

'I've run away from a little old woman,

A little old man,

A barn full of threshers,

A field full of mowers,

A cow,

And I can run away from you, I can!

Run, run as fast as you can!

You can't catch me,

I'm the Gingerbread Man!'

The pig ran after the Gingerbread Man, but he couldn't
catch him.

The little Gingerbread Man ran until he came to a river. He didn't know how to swim and couldn't get across.

A sly fox was sitting by the river and saw the Gingerbread Man standing there. 'Do you want to get across the river little man?' asked the fox. 'Jump on my tail and I'll carry you across.'

'He won't be able to reach me from his tail,' thought the Gingerbread Man. 'I'll be safe there.'

The Gingerbread Man climbed on the fox's tail and the fox started swimming across the river.

A little way across, the fox's tail started drooping into the water and the Gingerbread Man was in danger of getting wet.

'You're too heavy for my tail,' said the fox. 'Get on my back.'

So the Gingerbread Man climbed up on to the fox's back.

A little further across, the fox's back started to sag. 'You're too heavy for my back,' said the fox. 'Sit on my nose.'

So the Gingerbread Man climbed on to the fox's nose.

As soon as he reached the riverbank, the fox tossed his head, throwing the Gingerbread Man into the air. He snapped his mouth shut and ate the Gingerbread Man up in one mouthful. The Gingerbread Man was all gone!

'Delicious!' said the sly fox.

LITTLE
RED RIDING
HOOD

Once upon a time there lived a girl named Little Red Riding Hood. She was called that because she loved to wear a hooded cape of red velvet that her Grandmother had made for her.

One day, her mother said, 'Come Little Red Riding Hood. Your poor Grandmother is ill. I need you to take this bread and cheese to her. Remember, you must stay on the path and go straight there.'

Little Red Riding Hood put the bread and cheese in a basket and set off to her Grandmother's house. Her Grandmother lived on the other side of a nearby wood.

As she was going through the wood, Little Red Riding Hood met a Wolf. The Wolf took one look at Little Red Riding Hood and thought how tasty she looked, but he didn't dare eat her because there were some woodsmen nearby.

'Good day, little maid,' said the Wolf. 'Where are you off to on such a fine day?'

Little Red Riding Hood, who didn't know that it was dangerous to talk to the Wolf, said, 'I am going to see Grandmother. She isn't well, so I am taking her this bread and cheese.'

'Where does she live?' asked the Wolf.

'Why, just through the wood, under the three oak trees,' replied Little Red Riding Hood.

The Wolf thought for a minute, and then said, 'See how pretty the flowers are about here? I am sure your Grandmother would love to see them.'

Little Red Riding Hood looked at the flowers and thought, 'Maybe I should take Grandmother a fresh posy. She'd be so pleased and it is early in the day, so I will still get there in good time.'

'That's a good idea,' said Little Red Riding Hood, and she ran from the path to look for flowers to pick.

Meanwhile, the Wolf ran ahead along the path to Grandmother's house under the three oak trees and knocked on the door.

'Who is there?' asked Grandmother.

'Little Red Riding Hood,' replied the Wolf, imitating her voice, 'with bread and cheese.'

'Come in,' called out Grandmother. 'I am too weak to come to the door.'

The Wolf lifted the latch and went inside. He ate Grandmother in one mouthful. Then he put on a set of her nightclothes and a nightcap, lay down in her bed and drew the curtains so that the room was quite dim.

Little Red Riding Hood gathered a lovely posy of flowers and continued on her way to Grandmother's house. When she got there, she knocked on the door. A husky voice called out, 'Who is there?'

'Little Red Riding Hood, with bread and cheese,' she replied.

'Come in,' called the Wolf. 'I am too weak to come to the door.'

Little Red Riding Hood lifted the latch and went inside. It was quite dark but she could see the shape of her Grandmother under the bedclothes, her nightcap pulled low over her face.

'Put the bread down and come and sit with me,' said the Wolf.

Little Red Riding Hood sat by the bed. She was surprised at how Grandmother looked in her nightclothes.

'Oh Grandmother, what big ears you have!' she said.

'All the better to hear you with,' was the reply.

'Oh Grandmother, what big arms you have!' she said.

'All the better to hug you with,' was the reply.

'Oh Grandmother, what big eyes you have!' she said.

'All the better to see you with,' was the reply.

'Oh Grandmother, what big teeth you have!' she said.

'All the better to eat you with!' was the reply, and the Wolf bounded out of bed and ate Little Red Riding Hood in one mouthful.

The Wolf felt sleepy after his big feast, so he lay down again in the bed and fell asleep. He started to snore very loudly.

Just then, a huntsman who lived nearby was passing the house. 'Goodness, how loudly the old woman is snoring,' he thought. 'She sounds very unwell. I might just pop my head in and see if she is all right.'

The huntsman looked inside and saw the Wolf lying in the bed, fast asleep, his belly full. The huntsman, who had long been hunting the Wolf, took his rifle and was about to shoot when it occurred to him that the Wolf might have eaten the old woman, and she still might be saved.

He took his hunting knife and cut open the Wolf's stomach. Little Red Riding Hood sprang out, saying, 'Oh, it was so dark in there!' Then Grandmother slowly climbed out, shaky but alive.

The huntsman went off with the Wolf's skin and Grandmother and Little Red Riding Hood shared the bread and cheese. 'Never again will I leave the path to run into the woods when my mother has forbidden it,' Little Red Riding Hood thought to herself as she finished her delicious food.

THE THREE WISHES

Once upon a time there was a poor Woodcutter and his wife who lived next to a great forest. Every day, the Woodcutter went into the forest to cut timber.

One day, the Woodcutter was working in a clearing. He had marked out a huge old oak tree, which looked like it would make many planks of wood. He went up to the tree with his axe in his hand. He swung the axe back as though he were about to fell the tree with one mighty stroke.

But the Woodcutter hadn't even made one cut when he heard a small, pitiful voice calling to him. There before him hovered a tiny Fairy, who prayed and begged him to spare the oak tree, as it was her home.

The Woodcutter was so astonished that he could not utter a word. But at last he overcame his wonder and found his tongue. 'Well,' he said, 'if it's your home then I can't cut it down. I'll do as you ask.'

'You've done more for yourself than you know,' replied the Fairy. 'To show I'm not ungrateful, I'll grant you your next three wishes.'

Then the Fairy vanished, leaving the Woodcutter wondering if he had been dreaming. He slung the axe over his shoulder and started for home.

When he got there, he sat by the fire and called to his wife. He told her what had happened, and she began to formulate all sorts of grand plans. However, realising they should act prudently, she said, 'Let's not spoil anything by being impatient. We must think things over carefully. Let's put our first wish off until tomorrow and sleep on it.'

'You are right,' said the Woodcutter. He sat back in his chair by the fire and warmed himself. 'What a fine blaze!' the Woodcutter said.

'Indeed,' replied his wife. 'I wish we had some sausages. It would be nice to enjoy them by the fire.'

Scarcely had the Woodcutter's wife finished speaking when she and her husband saw a link of sausages appear down the chimney. The Woodcutter cried out in alarm, but then realised that this was the result of the foolish wish that his wife had made. He began to scold her.

'You fool!' he cried. 'To think you might have wished for a kingdom, with gold, pearls, rubies, diamonds, fine clothes, whatever you desire! And all you wish for are sausages!'

'Alas,' replied the Woodcutter's wife. 'I've made a very bad choice. I'll do better next time.'

'Yes, you will!' exclaimed the Woodcutter. 'You couldn't have done any worse! Only a fool would have wished for sausages. A curse on all sausages! I wish a sausage was hanging from your nose!'

In a flash, the wish was answered and a sausage fastened itself on the end of her nose. The Woodcutter's wife screamed and tried to pull it off, but it was stuck. Then the Woodcutter tried to pull it off, but it was stuck fast. Then they both tried but the sausage showed no sign of moving and they were in danger of pulling her nose off.

The Woodcutter's wife cried and sobbed. 'You make a wish,' she told her husband.

'No, you make a wish,' replied the Woodcutter, who also started to cry at the state of his poor wife's nose.

They had one wish left. What were they to wish for? They might wish for something very grand, but what use was all the finery in the world if the mistress of the house had a sausage stuck to the end of her nose?

Then the Woodcutter decided he would make the best use he could of the last wish and said, 'I wish my wife was rid of the sausage from her nose.'

And the next moment the sausage fell off her nose and into a dish on the table! They were so relieved that they danced around the room for joy and then ate the sausage, which was the finest sausage anyone could wish for.

The Woodcutter and his wife didn't mind that they weren't going to ride around in a golden coach or dress in fine silk. They realised that it is much better to enjoy eating a sausage than to have one attached to your nose for the rest of your life.

RAPUNZEL

Once upon a time there lived a couple who were going to have a child. They had a little window at the back of their house that looked out onto a lovely garden. The garden was surrounded by a high wall and no one dared enter it, for it belonged to a powerful Witch.

One day, the wife stood at the window and saw a garden bed full of the finest lettuce. When she realised she couldn't have any, she pined away and became pale and weak.

'Oh,' she moaned, 'if I can't have some lettuce to eat from the garden, I shall die.'

The man, who loved her dearly, thought, 'I should fetch her some lettuce, no matter what the cost.'

At sunset, the husband climbed over the wall into the Witch's garden. He quickly gathered a handful of lettuce leaves and returned with them to his wife. They tasted so good that her longing for the forbidden food grew stronger than ever. If she were to have any peace of mind, her husband would have to fetch her some more.

When the sun set, he climbed over the wall. Then he drew back in terror, for standing before him was the old Witch.

'How dare you steal my lettuce like a common thief?' she demanded. 'You shall suffer for your foolhardiness!'

'Please, spare me!' he implored. 'My wife saw your lettuce from her window. She had such a desire for it that she would certainly have died if she could not have a taste.'

Then the Witch grew a little less angry. She said, 'If that's so, you may take as much lettuce as you like, but on one condition: you will give me your child when it is born. I will look after it like a mother.' In his terror, the man agreed.

As soon as the child was born, it was taken away by the Witch. She named the girl Rapunzel, which is the name of the lettuce the child's mother so desired. Rapunzel was the most beautiful child under the sun. When she was twelve years old, the Witch shut her up in a tower in the middle of a great wood. The tower had no stairs or doors and only a small window at the very top. When the Witch wanted to get in, she stood under the window and called out:

'Rapunzel, Rapunzel, let down your hair.'

Rapunzel had beautiful, long hair as fine as spun gold. When she heard the Witch calling, she let her braid of hair fall down and the old Witch climbed up it to the top of the tower.

One day, a few years later, a Prince was riding through the wood. As he approached the tower, he heard someone singing so beautifully that he stopped and listened, entranced. It was Rapunzel, who, in her loneliness, passed the time by singing songs, her lovely voice ringing out into the forest.

The Prince longed to see who was singing, but there was no door in the tower. He was so captivated that he returned to the wood every day. One day, he was listening from behind a tree when he saw the old Witch. He heard her call out:

'Rapunzel, Rapunzel, let down your hair.'

Rapunzel let down her hair and the Witch climbed up. 'If that's the way into the tower, I'll try my luck,' thought the Prince.

The next day at sunset, the Prince went to the foot of the tower and cried out:

'Rapunzel, Rapunzel, let down your hair.'

As soon as Rapunzel let it down, the Prince climbed up.

At first Rapunzel was terribly frightened by this young man she had never met before. However, the Prince spoke to her kindly and gently. He told her that his heart had been so touched by her singing that he could not rest until he had met her. Very soon Rapunzel forgot her fear.

The Prince visited her often. When he asked her to marry him, she said, 'I will gladly marry you, only how am I to get out of the tower?' She thought for a moment and said, 'Every time you visit, bring a skein of silk. I will make a ladder. When it is finished, I will climb down and you can take me away on your horse.'

The Prince visited every evening because the Witch came during the day. The Witch knew nothing about this until one day Rapunzel, not thinking, asked the Witch, 'Why are you so much harder to pull up than the Prince? He is always with me in a moment.'

'Wicked child!' cried the Witch. 'I thought I had hidden you from the whole world, yet you have still managed to trick me!'

She grabbed Rapunzel's beautiful hair and picked up a pair of scissors. Snip! Snap! Off it came! The beautiful golden plait lay on the floor. The Witch was so cruel that she sent Rapunzel to a lonely desert to live in misery.

That evening, the Witch fastened the braid of hair to a hook in the window. The Prince came and called out:

'Rapunzel, Rapunzel, let down your hair!'

The Witch threw the plait down, and the Prince climbed up. Instead of his dear Rapunzel, he found the old Witch, laughing mockingly, 'Ha ha! You thought to find a pretty bird but she has flown away and won't sing any more! You will never see her again!'

The Prince was overcome with grief. In his despair, he jumped from the tower. He escaped with his life, but he fell in a thorn bush. The sharp thorns pierced his eyes and he could no longer see.

The Prince wandered, blind and miserable, through the forest. He ate nothing but roots and berries, and wept and mourned the loss of his beloved bride. He wandered like this from place to place for many years, as wretched and unhappy as it was possible to be.

At last, the poor blind Prince wandered to the desert where Rapunzel was living. He was roaming about in despair when he suddenly heard a familiar voice singing. The Prince eagerly followed the lovely sound, and when he was quite close, Rapunzel saw him and recognised him.

Rapunzel threw her arms around the Prince's neck and wept for joy at seeing him again and for sorrow at his poor sightless eyes. But then two of her tears fell into his eyes. Immediately, the Prince's eyes became clear and he could see as well as he had ever done.

The Prince led Rapunzel to his kingdom, where they were received and welcomed with great joy and relief. They were married and lived happily ever after.

THE
LITTLE MATCH
GIRL

It was nearly dark on the last night of the year. It was bitterly cold and the snow was falling fast. In the cold and the dark, a poor little girl roamed through the streets. Her head and feet were bare.

She did have on a pair of slippers when she left home, although they were not much use. They were very large, as they had belonged to her mother. The poor little thing had lost them as she was running across the street, trying to avoid two carriages that were speeding along at a terrible rate. One of the slippers she could not find and the other had been seized by a boy, who ran away with it. So the little girl went on with her naked feet, which were quite red and blue from the cold.

The girl carried a number of matches in her apron pocket and had a bundle of them in her hands. She was a match seller. No one had bought any matches from her the whole day, nor had anyone given her a penny. She crept along, shivering with the cold and hunger, a picture of misery. The snowflakes fell on her long, fair hair, which hung in wet curls on her shoulders, but she ignored them.

Instead, she looked at the lights shining from every window and smelled the delicious aroma of roast goose that hung in the air, for it was New Year's Eve. In a corner between two houses, she sank down and huddled into herself. She pulled her bare feet in underneath her, but she could not keep out the cold.

She dared not go home, for she had not sold any matches and had no money for her family. Besides, it was nearly as cold at home as here, for there was only the roof to cover them. It was full of holes and cracks through which the wind howled, even though they had tried to fill the largest holes with straw and rags.

The Match Girl's hands were almost numb with cold. Oh! A burning match might give her some small comfort, if only she dared to take a single one out of the bundle and strike it against the wall.

She drew a match out of the bundle. 'Scratch!' How it spluttered and blazed as it burned! The flame was warm and bright, like a little candle, as she held her hand over it. It was a wonderful light!

It seemed to the little Match Girl that she was sitting beside a large iron stove, with polished brass feet and a polished chimney. How the fire burned! Her little corner seemed so beautifully snug as the little girl stretched out her feet as though to warm them, when suddenly the little flame went out. The stove vanished and she was left with the remains of the match in her hand.

She struck another match on the wall. It burst into flame brightly. It seemed that where its light fell on the wall, it became as transparent as a veil and she could see into the room. The table was spread with a snow-white tablecloth, on which stood a splendid china dinner set and a steaming roast goose, stuffed with apples and dried plums. And what was even more wonderful was that the goose jumped down from the dish and danced across the room to the little girl.

Then the match went out and there was nothing left but the thick, cold, damp wall in front of her.

She lit another match and found herself sitting under a beautiful Christmas tree. It was even larger and more magnificently decorated than the one that she had seen through the glass door of a rich shopkeeper's house. Thousands of candles burned in the green branches and brightly coloured pictures, like ones she had seen in shop windows, looked down on her. The little girl stretched out her hand to them, and the match went out.

The Christmas lights rose higher until she saw that they were the stars in the sky. Then she saw a star fall, leaving a long trail of fire. 'Someone has just died,' thought the little girl, for her old grandmother, the only person who had ever loved her and who was now no more, had told her that when a star falls, a soul goes up to Heaven.

She struck another match against the wall and the light shone around her. In the brightness stood her old grandmother, bright and radiant, so mild and full of love.

'Grandmother!' she cried out. 'Oh, take me with you! I know you will go away when the match goes out. You will vanish like the warm stove, the roast goose and the magnificent Christmas tree.'

She struck the whole bundle of matches against the wall, for she wished to keep her grandmother there. The matches glowed with a light that was brighter than the sun at noon and her grandmother had never appeared so beautiful and so tall. She took the little girl in her arms and they flew upwards into a place of brightness and joy, where there was neither hunger, nor cold, nor pain.

In the corner in the dawn light, there lay the poor little Match Girl, with pale cheeks and a joyful smile, curled up near the wall. She was still holding the matches in her hand, one bundle of which was burnt.

'She tried to warm herself,' people said. No one could imagine the beautiful things she had seen or understand what splendour she had entered with her grandmother, on that cold New Year's Eve.

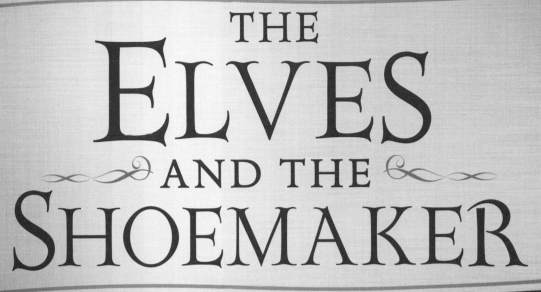

THE
ELVES
AND THE
SHOEMAKER

Once there lived a Shoemaker and his wife. They worked very hard and were very honest, but they were also very poor. They could not make enough money to live on and soon everything they had in the world was gone. All they had left was just enough leather to make one pair of shoes.

The poor Shoemaker cut out the leather and laid it out, ready to make into shoes early the next morning. 'Tomorrow, when it is sunny, I will work on them,' he told his wife. The good Shoemaker said his prayers and lay down to sleep.

The next morning, he went to start work on the shoes. However, to his wonder, he saw the shoes sitting there on the table, already finished. What an odd thing! The good man didn't know what to say or think. He looked at the workmanship on the shoes. They were so perfect, there was not a stitch wrong.

Soon a customer came in and asked to see the shoes. They suited him so well that he paid much more for them than was usual. The poor Shoemaker was able to buy enough leather to make two pairs of shoes. That evening he cut out the leather and laid it out, ready to work on the next morning.

When the Shoemaker got up the next day and went into his shop to start work, there were two finished pairs of shoes sitting there. Again, the work was that of a master. Soon some customers came in and bought the shoes, so that the shoemaker could buy enough leather to make four pairs. He cut out the leather and laid it out overnight. Sure enough, the next morning he awoke to find four pairs of shoes sitting there.

This continued on: the Shoemaker would cut out the leather in the evening and wake to find the shoes finished by daybreak. Soon the good Shoemaker's business was thriving.

One evening in winter, the Shoemaker and his wife were sitting by the fire talking together. The Shoemaker said, 'I should like to stay awake tonight and see who it is that comes and does my work for me.'

His wife thought that was an excellent idea. They lit the candle and then hid themselves behind a curtain in the corner of the room to see what would happen.

Right on the stroke of midnight, two little Elves dressed in ragged clothes with bare feet skipped in. They sat down on the Shoemaker's bench and picked up the cut-out leather. Their little fingers flew as their needles stitched back and forth and their little hammers rap-a-tap-tapped.

'Poor fellows! They must be so cold,' whispered the Shoemaker's wife, and indeed, they were shivering as they worked.

Soon, all the shoes sat ready on the bench. The two little Elves skipped and danced around the room and then they were gone.

The next morning, the Shoemaker said to his wife, 'I would so like to thank those good creatures for what they've done for us. What can we do for them?'

'Their clothes are so ragged and thin,' said the Shoemaker's wife. 'I will make them a warm woollen jacket, a shirt, a waistcoat and a pair of stockings and pantaloons each.'

The Shoemaker was very pleased with this idea. 'If you'll make them some clothes, I'll make them each a pair of shoes,' he said.

When everything was ready, instead of laying out the cut-out leather, they laid out the little outfits on the work table. Then the Shoemaker and his wife hid behind the curtain to see what the little Elves would do.

At the stroke of midnight, the two Elves skipped in. When they went to sit at the table, they saw the clothes and shoes lying there ready for them. They laughed and chuckled in delight and clapped their hands with joy.

They dressed themselves in their new outfits and danced and capered about the room. As they danced, they sang:

'Now we are so fine to see,

No longer need we cobblers be!'

Then they skipped out the door.

The good Shoemaker and his wife never saw the two little Elves
again, but they lived long and happy lives and good luck was with
them always.

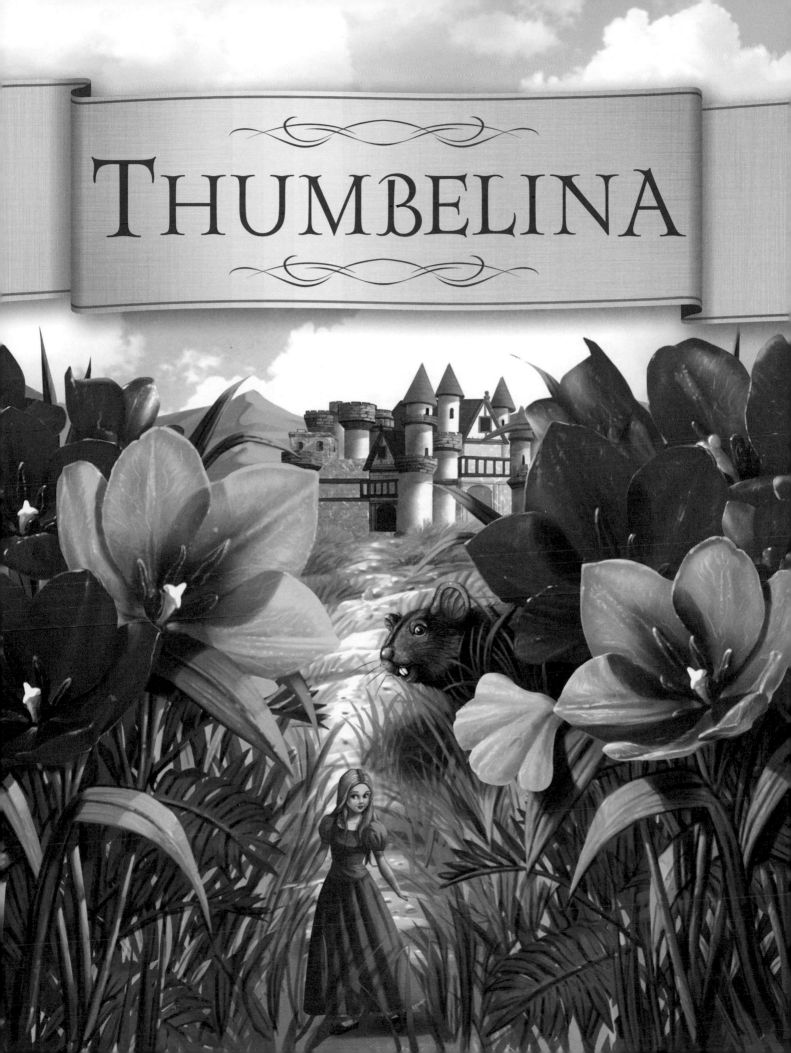

Thumbelina

There was once a woman who wished to have a child. She went to a fairy, and said, 'I would like to have a child so much. Can you help me?'

'Oh, that is easy,' said the fairy. 'Here is some special barley. Put it into a flower-pot and see what happens.'

The woman went home and planted the barley. Immediately a handsome flower grew, its petals tightly closed like a bud. As the woman watched in astonishment, the flower opened to reveal a graceful little maiden. She was barely half as long as a thumb, so the woman named her Thumbelina. Her bed was a walnut shell with a violet-petal mattress and a rose-petal quilt.

One night, a large, ugly toad crept through the window and saw Thumbelina sleeping in her walnut shell. 'What a pretty little wife for my son,' said the toad, and she took the shell to the stream where she lived with her son.

'We will put her on a water-lily leaf in the middle of the stream so she won't escape,' said the toad to her son. When Thumbelina woke the next morning she began to cry, for she did not know where she was or how to get home.

The old toad swam out to the leaf with her ugly son and said, 'Here is my son. He will be your husband.'

Then they left Thumbelina alone on the water-lily leaf, where she sat and wept. She could not bear to think of life with the ugly toad.

The fish in the stream felt sorry that Thumbelina should have to live with the ugly toads so they surrounded the stalk of the leaf and gnawed it through. The water-lily leaf floated down the stream carrying Thumbelina to faraway lands. Thumbelina was glad, for the toad could not reach her now. She lived by the river and the birds sweetly sang to her.

Summer and autumn passed and then came the long, cold winter. The birds who had sung to her flew away, and the trees and flowers withered. She was dreadfully cold, for her clothes were torn. It began to snow and she shivered with cold and hunger.

One day, while searching for food, Thumbelina came to the cottage of a field-mouse. She knocked on the door.

'You poor little creature,' said the field-mouse when she saw the starving girl. 'Come in and share my dinner.' She quickly came to like Thumbelina and said, 'You can stay with me all winter if you keep my rooms clean.' Thumbelina agreed and was very happy.

'My neighbour is a very rich mole,' said the field-mouse. 'If you had him for a husband you would be well provided for.'

The mole was indeed rich, but he was also quite disagreeable and did not like the sun. The field-mouse insisted Thumbelina sing to him, and the mole fell in love with her sweet voice. He dug a passage from the field-mouse's house to his burrow and encouraged them to visit whenever they liked.

One evening, the mole and Thumbelina were walking together when they came upon a swallow that had died of cold. The mole said, 'How miserable it must be to be a bird! They do nothing but sing in the summer and die of hunger in the winter.'

Thumbelina said nothing. 'Perhaps this bird sang to me sweetly in the summer,' she thought.

That night Thumbelina could not sleep, so she got out of bed and wove a carpet of hay. She carried it to the bird and spread it over him so that he might lie warmly in the cold earth. 'Farewell, pretty bird,' she said.

Thumbelina laid her head on the bird's breast and was surprised when his heart went 'thump, thump'. He was not dead, only numb from the cold and the warm carpet had restored him to life.

The next morning Thumbelina stole out to see him. He was very weak and could barely open an eye to look at her.

'Stay in your warm bed and I will take care of you,' she said. With much care and love Thumbelina nursed him in secret for the whole winter.

When spring came, the swallow bade farewell to Thumbelina. He asked if she would go with him but Thumbelina knew it would make the field-mouse very sad if she left her and said, 'No, I cannot.'

'Farewell then, little maiden,' said the swallow and he flew out into the sunshine.

Soon afterwards, the field-mouse took Thumbelina aside and said, 'You are going to be married to the mole as soon as summer is over.' Thumbelina wept at the thought. Every morning and evening she crept out to see the blue sky. She wished to see her dear swallow again but he had flown far away.

The day approached when the mole was to take Thumbelina away to live with him. She went to say goodbye to the sun. 'Farewell bright sun,' she cried, curling her arm around a red flower. 'Greet the swallow for me, if you should see him again.'

Suddenly she heard a loud 'tweet, tweet!' from above. She looked up and saw the swallow. 'Winter is coming,' he said. 'Now will you fly with me to warmer lands?'

'I will,' said Thumbelina, and she climbed on to the bird's back. The swallow flew over forests and high above mountains, leaving the mole and the field-mouse far behind.

At last they came to a blue lake. Beside it, surrounded by flowers, stood a palace of white marble. The swallow laid Thumbelina gently in a beautiful blossom.

'I live in a nest beneath this castle's tallest turret but you shall live here,' said the swallow with a knowing smile.

On the flower stood a man, as tiny as Thumbelina, wearing a gold crown and delicate wings. A tiny man or woman lived in every flower and he was the King of them all. The little King thought her the prettiest maiden he had ever seen. He asked her to marry him and to be Queen of all the flowers.

Thumbelina happily agreed. For the wedding she was given a lovely pair of wings, which were fastened to her shoulders so she could fly from flower to flower as the little swallow sang a wedding song.

'Farewell, farewell,' said the swallow when it was time to return to the forest for summer.

There he had a nest over the window of a house where a writer of fairytales lived. The swallow sang, 'Tweet, tweet,' and from his song came this story.

THE
SHEPHERDESS
AND THE
CHIMNEY SWEEP

Once upon a time in a great big house, there stood an old wooden cupboard, quite black with age. It was covered from top to bottom with carved roses and tulips. Strange scrolls were drawn on it, and in the middle of the scrolls, little stags' heads with antlers peeped out.

In the centre of the cupboard door was the carved figure of a man. He had a wide grin on his face, goat's legs, little horns and a long beard. The children of the house called him 'Major-General-Field-Sergeant-Commander Billy Goat's Legs.' It was a very difficult name to pronounce and there are very few who have ever received such a title, but it seemed incredible how he ever came to be carved at all. Yet there he was.

Major-General-Field-Sergeant-Commander Billy Goat's Legs looked out at a table. On the table stood a very pretty little Shepherdess made of china. She wore a gilded hat and carried a gilded crook and looked very bright and pretty.

Close by her stood a little Chimney Sweep. His dirty clothes were as black as coal and he was also made of china. He held a ladder and his face was fair and rosy. Indeed, that was a mistake by the china makers, as it should have had some dirty marks on it.

The Chimney Sweep and the Shepherdess had been placed side by side. Standing so close, they decided to become engaged to each other. They were very well suited, as they were made of the same sort of china and were equally fragile.

Close by stood an old man made of china who could nod his head. He was three times as large as they were and was also made of china. He pretended that he was the Shepherdess's grandfather, although he could not prove it. When Major-General-Field-Sergeant-Commander Billy Goat's Legs asked for permission to marry the little Shepherdess, he nodded his head.

'You will have a husband,' said the old china man. 'He has a cupboard full of silver plates, locked up in secret drawers.'

'I won't go into the dark cupboard!' said the little Shepherdess. 'I have heard that he has eleven china wives in there already.'

'You shall be the twelfth,' said the old china man. 'Tonight you shall be married.' And he nodded his head and fell asleep.

The little Shepherdess cried and looked at the china Chimney Sweep. 'I beg you,' she said. 'Go out into the wide world with me, for I cannot stay here.'

'I will do whatever you wish,' said the little Chimney Sweep. 'Let us leave immediately. I can work and look after you.'

'If only we were safely down from the table!' she said. 'I shall not be happy until we are really out in the world.'

The little Chimney Sweep comforted her. He brought his little ladder to help and they managed to reach the floor. When they looked at the cupboard, they saw it was in an uproar. The carved stags pushed out their heads and raised their antlers. Major-General-Field-Sergeant-Commander Billy Goat's Legs cried out, 'They are running away! They are running away!'

The two were frightened, so they jumped into the drawer of the window-seat. In there were several packs of cards and a doll's theatre, where a comedy was being performed. All the queens of hearts, spades, clubs and diamonds sat in the first row, fanning themselves. The play was about two lovers who weren't allowed to marry, and the Shepherdess wept because it reminded her of her own story.

'I cannot bear it,' she said. 'We must get out of the drawer.'

When they reached the floor, they saw the old china man was awake. He shook his whole body until he tipped over and fell down. 'The old china man is coming!' cried the little Shepherdess in fright. 'There is nothing left for us but to go out into the wide world.'

When the Chimney Sweep saw that she was quite determined, he said, 'I'll take you through the stove and up the chimney. We shall soon climb too high for anyone to reach us and we'll go through the hole in the top out into the wide world.'

The Chimney Sweep led the Shepherdess to the stove door. 'It looks very dark,' she said in a worried voice. But she found the courage to go in with him.

'Now we are in the chimney,' he said. 'Look, there is a beautiful star shining above us!'

A real star shone down on them, as if it wanted to show them the way. They crept and clambered on. It was frightfully steep but the Chimney Sweep helped the Shepherdess and they climbed higher and higher. At last they reached the top of the chimney.

They sat down, for they were very tired. The sky, with all its stars, was over their heads, and below were the roofs of the town. They could see for a very long way out into the wide world. The poor little Shepherdess leaned her head on the Chimney Sweep's shoulder and wept. The world was so different to what she expected.

'This is too much,' she said. 'It is too large. Oh, I wish I were safe back on the table. I shall never be happy until I am safe back there. Please take me back, if you love me.'

The Chimney Sweep tried to reason with her. He spoke of the old china man and Major-General-Field-Sergeant-Commander Billy Goat's Legs, but she sobbed bitterly and kissed her little Chimney Sweep until he did what she asked.

With a great deal of trouble, they climbed down the chimney and crept through the stove. Then they stood in the dark fire-box and listened through the door to hear what was going on in the room.

As it was all quiet, they peeped out. The old china man lay on the floor. He had broken into three pieces when he fell off the table. His back had separated into two and his head had rolled away from his body.

'This is terrible!' said the little Shepherdess. 'My poor old grandfather is broken to pieces, and it is our fault.' She wrung her little hands.

'He can be riveted back together,' said the Chimney Sweep. 'If they cement his back and put a rivet in it, he will be as good as new and will be able to say as many disagreeable things to us as ever.'

'Do you think so?' she asked. They climbed up to the table and stood in their old places. 'I wish grandfather could be repaired,' said the Shepherdess, sadly.

She had her wish. The family had the china man's back mended and a strong rivet put through his neck. He looked as good as new, but he could no longer nod his head.

'Am I to marry her or not?' asked Major-General-Field-Sergeant-Commander Billy Goat's Legs.

The Chimney Sweep and the little Shepherdess looked at the old china man, as they were afraid he might nod, but he couldn't because of the rivet. And so the little china people remained together and were glad of the rivet. They loved each other until they were finally broken into pieces many years later.

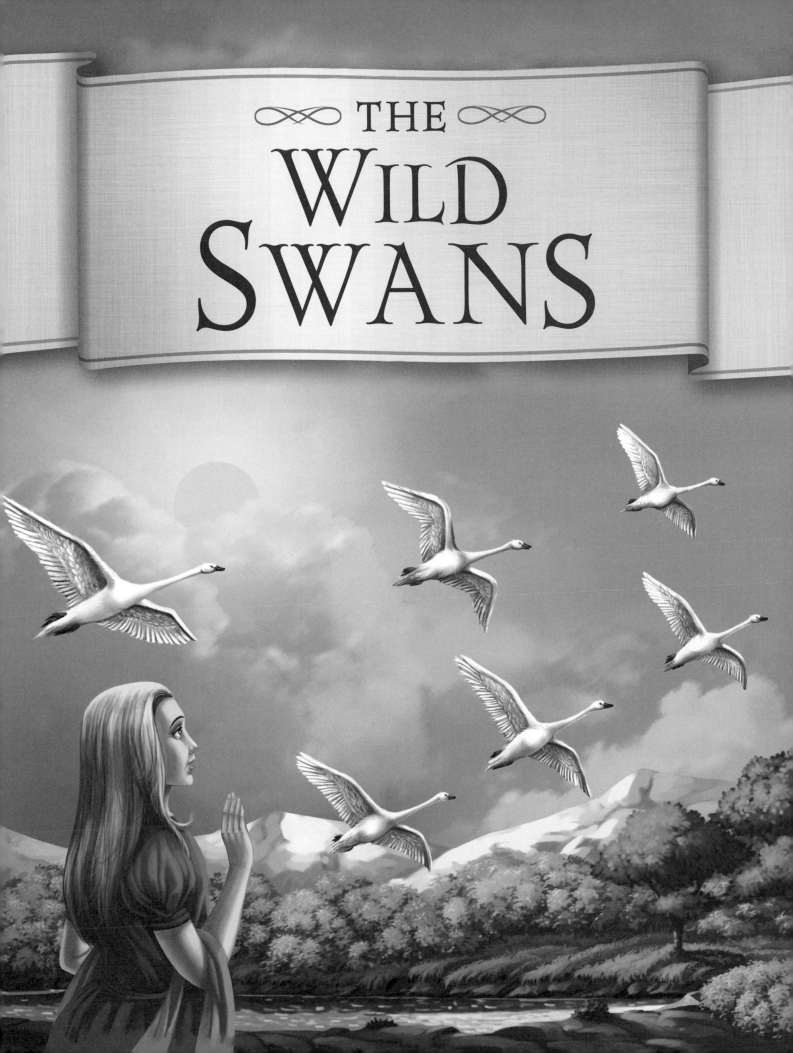

Once upon a time there lived a King. One day he was out hunting in a great wood. When evening came he stopped and realised that he was lost. Suddenly he saw an old woman coming towards him. She was a witch.

'My good woman,' the King said. 'Can you show me the way out of the wood?'

'Yes I can,' she answered. 'But there is one condition. I have a beautiful daughter. Marry her and make her Queen and I will show you the way out.' The King reluctantly agreed.

The old woman led him to her daughter. Although she was very beautiful, the King could not look at her without a feeling of dread. However, he could not break his word, so he helped the maiden on to his horse.

The old woman showed him the way out of the wood and he was soon home at his royal castle, where the wedding was held.

The King's first wife had died, leaving seven children: six boys and one girl, whom he loved more than anything in the world. Afraid their new stepmother might do them some harm, he took the children to live in a lonely castle in the middle of a forest. The road to the castle was hidden so the King used a magic ball of yarn to find it. When he threw it down, it unrolled itself and showed him the way.

The King went so often to see his children that the new Queen grew angry. She wanted to know why he went out alone into the wood so often. She bribed his servants and they told her about the secret castle and the magic ball of yarn.

The Queen did not rest until she had found the yarn. Then she made some white silk shirts with a charm sewn in each of them. When the King was out hunting, she took the shirts into the wood and used the ball of yarn to show her the way to the castle. The children saw someone in the distance but thought it was their father and ran to meet him.

The wicked Queen threw the shirts over the children. When the shirts touched their bodies, they changed into swans and flew away. The Queen went home very pleased, but as the daughter had not run out with her brothers, the Queen knew nothing about her.

The next day the King went to see his children, but he found no one but his daughter.

The girl told him about her brothers turning into swans. The King grieved, but he didn't know that it was his Queen who had done this. He tried to take his daughter back to the royal castle, but she begged the King to let her stay one more night. She thought, 'I must go and look for my brothers.'

When night came, she went into the wood. She ran all night and the next day until she was in another land.

At last she came to a hut with six beds. She crept underneath one and rested on the hard floor. When sunset was near, she saw six swans fly in the window. When they landed, they turned into her brothers.

The boys were delighted to see their sister, but their joy did not last long.

'You can't stay here,' they said. 'This is a robbers' den.'

'Can't you protect me?' asked their sister.

'No,' her brothers answered. 'We are only human every evening for a quarter of an hour.'

Their sister wept and asked, 'Can nothing be done to set you free?'

'No,' they replied. 'It would be too much to ask. For six years you could not speak or laugh. During that time you would have to make six shirts out of nettles. If you spoke before they were finished, the spell would not be broken.' Suddenly, they changed into swans and flew out the window.